THE

BOOK

Retold by Rob Lloyd Jones

Based on the story by Rudyard Kipling

Illustrated by Shahar Kober

Once, a little boy became lost in a jungle... but luckily he was found by a kind wolf.

That night, the boy snuggled up in warm wolf fur.

"We shall call him Mowgli," decided the mother wolf.

Later, amber eyes glared into the den.

It was the vicious tiger Shere Khan.

"I smell a man cub," he snarled.

"GIVE HIM TO ME TO EAT!"

Shere Khan growled, but the wolves howled and chased him away.

The next evening, under a silver moon, the wolves' leader Akela decided that Mowgli would live with them.

Shere Khan watched from the shadows...

"One day," the tiger snarled, "I will have that man cub for lunch."

So Mowgli lived with the animals of the jungle.

He was protected by the wolves, and a big black panther called Bagheera.

Baloo, a friendly old bear, taught him to talk to animals.

By day, they walked and talked.
At night, they slept curled up
under trees and tangled vines.

Whispers about Mowgli the man cub spread through the jungle.

In the dead of night, some jealous monkeys crept close...

Hooting and howling, they
snatched Mowgli from his sleep.

"Baloo!" Mowgli yelled. "BAGHEERA!"

The monkeys shrieked louder, drowning
Mowgli's cries, as they swung
him from tree to tree.

They took Mowgli to an ancient
palace with cracked walls
and crumbling towers.

"This is our home," they chattered.
"Now it is yours too."

Baloo and Bagheera searched
for Mowgli, **day** after **day**,
through the hot, sweaty jungle.

Finally, they asked
a snake called Kaa.

Yesssss, I have sssseen the man cub.

He isss with the monkeysss
in the lossssst city.

Follow me... thisss way...

Bagheera and Baloo sneaked silently
to the palace...
and
then
they
POUNCED!

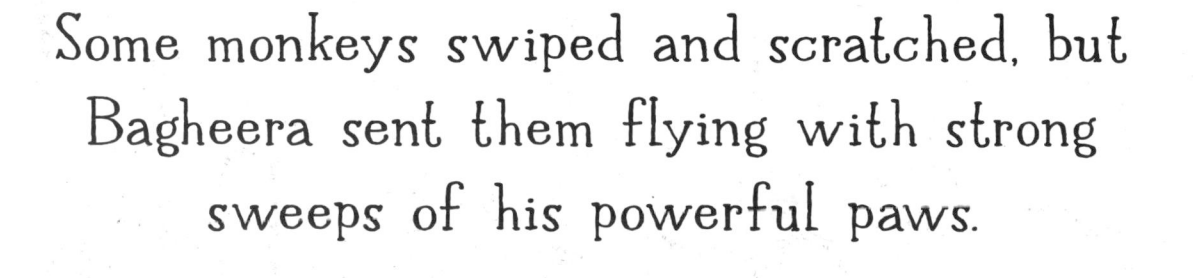

Some monkeys swiped and scratched, but
Bagheera sent them flying with strong
sweeps of his powerful paws.

The others took one look at Baloo and scattered.

None of them wanted to fight
a bear, not even for a man cub.

*A lucky man cub,
to have such good friendsss.*

Mowgli fell fast asleep as his friends carried him home. But still Bagheera worried...

"Shere Khan is after you," he warned Mowgli.

"Perhaps you should leave the jungle."

"But this is my home!" Mowgli replied.

As night fell, Mowgli crept to a village at the edge of the jungle, where a villager was cooking.

"Shere Khan may be big," Mowgli whispered,
"but I bet he's afraid of fire."

Mowgli raced back through the jungle and charged at
Shere Khan with sticks from the fire.
"GO AWAY!" he screamed.

The tiger shook with fear, but refused to flee.
"No, man cub," he snarled.
"Soon I will have you for my dinner."

"You must leave, Mowgli," Bagheera insisted.
"The jungle is too dangerous for you."
"Please let me stay," Mowgli begged.

But the wolves howled and Shere Khan
growled, and he knew that he had to go.

Trembling with fear and sadness, Mowgli returned to the human world.

The villagers were kind. They gave him a job herding buffaloes...

...and Mowgli laughed at their silly stories.

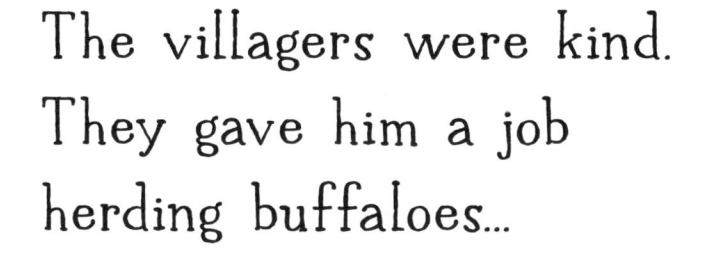

The village, though, was not his home.
At dusk he called to the wolves, and when
they came he was happy again.

"Shere Khan waits for you outside the village,"
the wolves warned. "You must never leave."

But Mowgli had a new plan...

The next morning, he led the buffaloes
into a ravine beyond the village.

"Shere Khan!" he called.
"It's me, the man cub
Mowgli."

A growl echoed along the ravine, and the tiger appeared.

"CHARGE!" Mowgli cried.

Shere Khan shrieked with terror at the sound
of the buffaloes' pounding hooves.

He turned and fled... and that was the last
anyone saw of that terrible tiger.

Mowgli scampered back to the jungle
and cried out in triumph.

"Shere Khan has gone!"

The wolves howled with pride and joy.
Their friend was back where he belonged.

Mowgli ran with them beside raging rivers and under towering trees. Every creature in the jungle heard his cry...

"I am Mowgli the man cub," he yelled, "and I am home!"

The Jungle Book was written by English author Rudyard Kipling over 120 years ago. The story is set in India, where Kipling lived when he was very young, and loved until he died.

Edited by Lesley Sims

Designed by Laura Nelson Norris

Digital imaging: Nick Wakeford

First published in 2019 by Usborne Publishing Ltd., Usborne House, 83-85 Saffron Hill, London EC1N 8RT, England. www.usborne.com Copyright © 2019, 2017 Usborne Publishing Ltd.